Admiral Richard Byrd was a pioneering polar explorer. In 1929, Byrd made aviation history with the first flight over the South Pole. His dog Igloo accompanied him on all of his explorations and was so popular that in 1931 a book titled *Igloo* was published about the dog's adventures with Byrd.

Meriwether Lewis was an American explorer best known for leading the Lewis and Clark expedition from 1804 to 1806. A Shawnee Indian once offered Lewis three beaver skins in trade for his Newfoundland, Seaman. Lewis said no to the bargain.

Billie Holiday was an American jazz singer and songwriter. Her nickname was Lady Day. Though she had quite a few dogs, the most well known was Mister, a boxer. One of Miss Holiday's friends called Mister "the best hang-out dog ever."

Orville Wright and his brother Wilbur were the inventors of the first successful airplane. Orville put up a fence by his lab so he could take his dog Scipio to work with him every day.

To the dogs in my life:
Duke, Tucker, Miss Puggy, Muffy, Emmie,
Marty, Mitzu, Sam, Toby, and Chloe
— E.S.

For Stela, Nicoli, and Snoopy
— G.V.

Text © 2011 Eileen Spinelli
Illustrations © 2011 Geraldo Valério

Published in 2011 by Eerdmans Books for Young Readers,
an imprint of Wm. B. Eerdmans Publishing Co.
2140 Oak Industrial Dr. NE
Grand Rapids, Michigan 49505
P.O. Box 163, Cambridge CB3 9PU U.K.

www.eerdmans.com/youngreaders

Manufactured at Tien Wah Press in Singapore in May 2011, first printing

11 12 13 14 15 16 17 18   9 8 7 6 5 4 3 2 1

Library of Congress Cataloging-in-Publication Data

Spinelli, Eileen.
Do you have a dog? / by Eileen Spinelli ; illustrated by Geraldo Valério.
p. cm.
Summary: Rhyming text describes some famous historical figures,
from Annie Oakley and Meriwether Lewis to Jackson Pollock and Billie Holiday,
and their beloved dogs. Includes facts about the people cited in the book.
ISBN 978-0-8028-5387-5 (alk. paper)
[1. Stories in rhyme. 2. Dogs — Fiction. 3. Biography — Fiction. 4. History — Fiction.]
I. Valério, Geraldo, 1970- ill. II. Title.
PZ8.3.S759Dnh 2011
[E] — dc22
2011005650

The illustrations were rendered in acrylic paint on watercolor paper.
The display type was set in Impress BT.
The text type was set in Gil Sans.

Do YOU HAVE A DOG?

Written by
Eileen Spinelli

Illustrated by
Geraldo Valério

Eerdmans Books for Young Readers

Grand Rapids, Michigan • Cambridge, U.K.

Do you have a dog?

A dog who wakes you, wants to play?

A dog who walks you every day?

Or one who leaps or fetches sticks?

A dog who does a lot of tricks?

Do **YOU** have a dog?

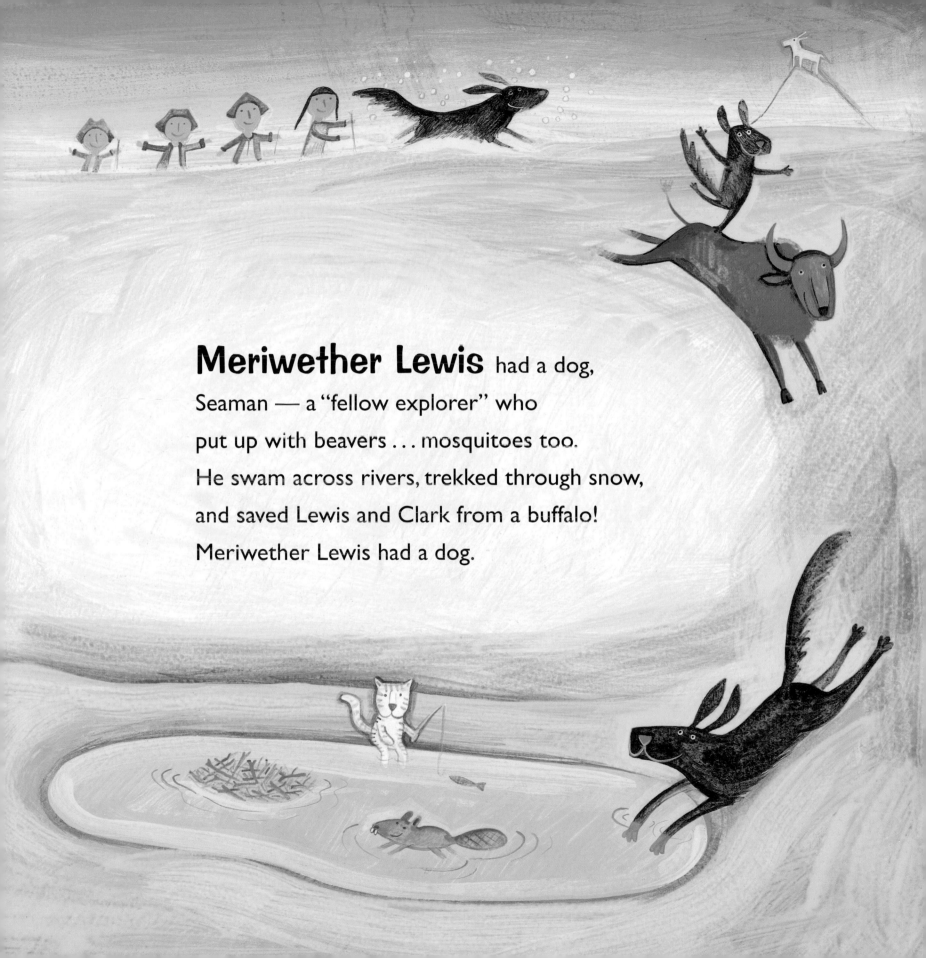

Meriwether Lewis had a dog,
Seaman — a "fellow explorer" who
put up with beavers . . . mosquitoes too.
He swam across rivers, trekked through snow,
and saved Lewis and Clark from a buffalo!
Meriwether Lewis had a dog.

Annie Oakley had a dog —
Dave. And, oh, what a thrill
were his tricks on the road with Buffalo Bill.
Of all the performers in the show "Wild West,"
Annie and Dave, they say, were the best.
Annie Oakley had a dog.

Admiral Richard Byrd had a dog —
Iggy — who kept Byrd warm,
a comfort in Antarctic storm.
Through blizzard, ice, and wild weather
the two holed up, good friends together.
Admiral Richard Byrd had a dog.

Billie Holiday had a dog
who sat backstage as he was told.
A dog named Mister — good as gold.
He seemed a rapt, contented thing
whenever he heard Billie sing.
Billie Holiday had a dog.

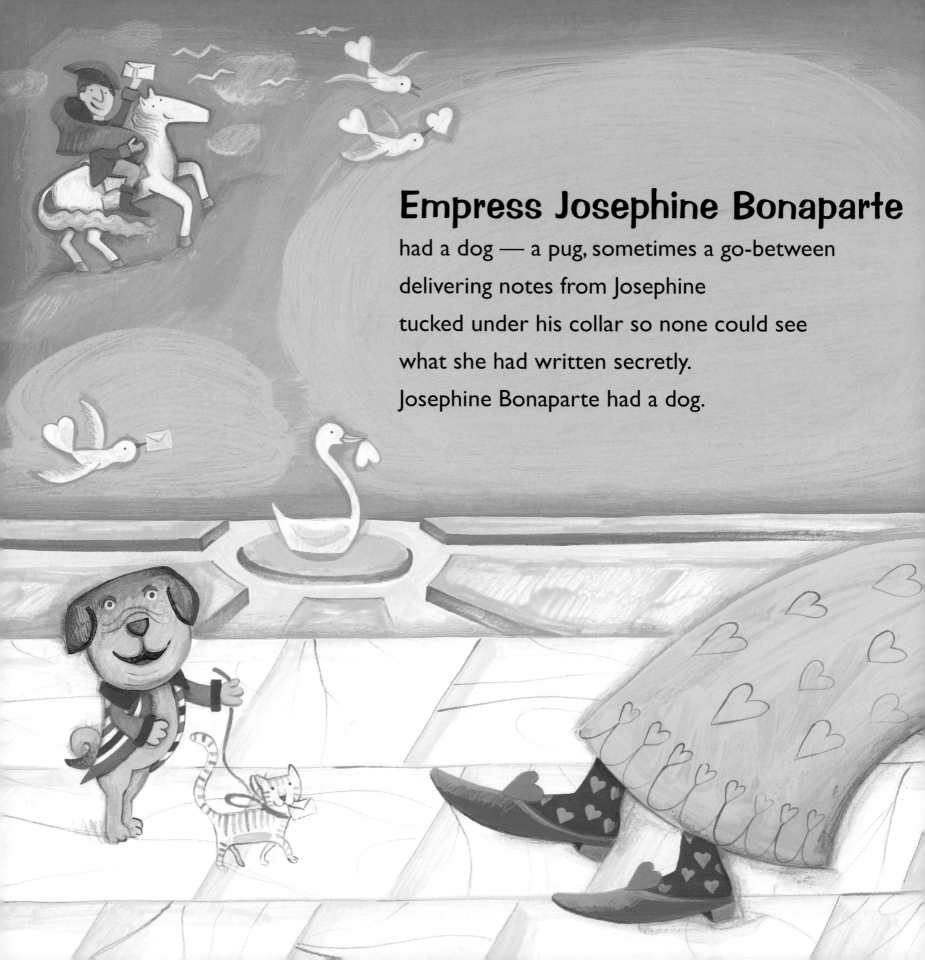

Empress Josephine Bonaparte

had a dog — a pug, sometimes a go-between
delivering notes from Josephine
tucked under his collar so none could see
what she had written secretly.
Josephine Bonaparte had a dog.

Agatha Christie had a dog.
He sat with her in her writing nook
and inspired a character for her book.
He on the rug and she in the chair —
they made a rather cozy pair.
Agatha Christie had a dog.

Jackson Pollock had a dog.
A gift to Pollock and his wife,
the poodle shared their country life,
romping out and clomping in
with paint on paws and mud on chin.
Jackson Pollock had a dog.

Franklin Delano Roosevelt

had a dog, Fala, who started every day
with a bone from the president's breakfast tray.
He went on jaunts by train and car —
ah, what a life with FDR.
Franklin Delano Roosevelt had a dog.

Helen Keller had a dog.
Sir Isaac Newton had one too.
Orville Wright had a dog.
Do YOU?

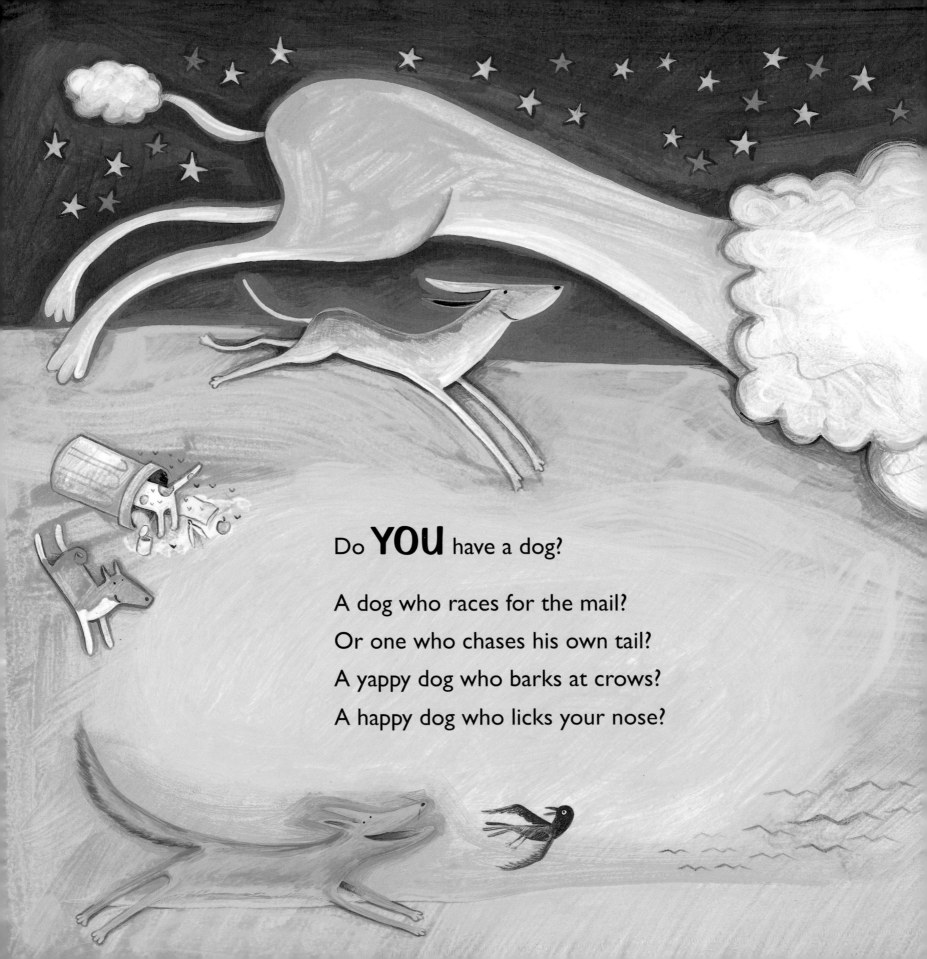

Do **YOU** have a dog?

A dog who races for the mail?
Or one who chases his own tail?
A yappy dog who barks at crows?
A happy dog who licks your nose?

A sloppy dog? A dainty one?

A dog who digs through trash for fun?

A dog who naps all afternoon?

Or howls at the autumn moon?

Do you have a dog?

A dog who's loving,

faithful,

true . . .

Or should I say,

Does a dog have **YOU**?

Agatha Christie was an English writer of detective stories. One of her novels, *Dumb Witness*, written in 1937, features a wirehaired terrier — just like her dog, Peter.

Jackson Pollock was an American abstract painter. He named his poodle Ahab after the captain in *Moby Dick* because Herman Melville was one of Pollock's favorite authors.

Helen Keller was an American author and lecturer. When she was two years old she became deaf and blind from an illness. As a child, Helen wanted to romp with her dog, Belle. But Belle preferred dozing by the fire.

Franklin Delano Roosevelt was the 32nd president of the United States, from 1933 to 1945. FDR enjoyed taking his dog Fala along on trips. Once on a ship in the West Indies Fala caused quite a stir by licking and tickling the sailors' feet.